Who Is King
In The Land Of Kachoo?

Written by Tina Scotford

Illustrated by Frans Groenewald

JACANA

In the heart of the land known as Kachoo
Lived a proud old lion who was the ruling king, too
He was golden and brave and of course very strong
And lazed in the sun all summer long

Now being ruled by a king that appeared to be lazy
Was driving some animals jealous and crazy!

Why should he get to wear the crown on his head
When he spent most days asleep in his bed?

While animals were gathered at the hole to drink water
The elephant, giraffe and baboon's middle daughter
A golden eagle flew to a tree
Making sure it was he they could see

He pounded his chest with his feathered wing
Then loudly screamed:

"Make me the king!

I, too, am strong and, look, I am gold
And if I may say so, I'm very bold

While soaring and gliding and flapping in flight
I can spot dinner with my perfect eyesight!"

The animals turned and looked at the tree
And nodded their heads; yes, they could see
The eagle was strong and very bold
His feathered body was covered in gold

But could he bring down a buck or a hog?
Or something more meaty than a slimy green frog?

The elephant, giraffe and baboon's middle child
Couldn't vote eagle the king of the wild
He was simply too small to come out the winner
While trying to bring down the animals' dinner

"What about me? I can be king,"
said spotted hyena from under the tree

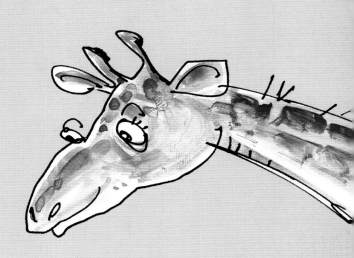

"I can bring down almost anything!
My coat is furry and golden in colour
And I'm very brave when I hunt with my brother!"

The elephant, giraffe and baboon's little girl
Stared at the hyena – could he give it a whirl?

Then one by one they shook their heads
"But your laughing sound is one we dread!
When we hear lion roar late in the night
We all run away, filled with fright
But we don't flee when we hear your laugh,"
Retorted the tallest orange giraffe

The elephant, giraffe and baboon's middle daughter
Continued to drink from the hole with the water

"I nominate my dad as king,"
said little baboon, while still drinking
"My dad is very, very strong
His teeth are nearly two inches long
The noises he makes sound just like a bark
That's sure to frighten animals away in the dark"

Elephant lowered his trunk to see baboon's baby face
"But does your dad have golden beauty, majesty and grace?
When lion talks or simply walks, he does so with great pride
His long limbs stretch out easily into an elegant stride

If your dad is as scary and as strong as you say
And can carry himself like a royal today
Then we'll gladly make him our new king
His praises from hilltops
we'll shout out and sing"

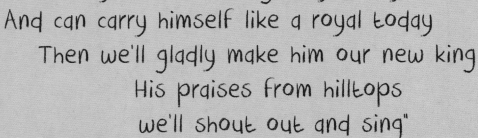

The baboon's little girl
his sweet middle daughter
Stared at her reflection bouncing back
from the water

"My dad is not golden, he's hairy and grey
And stretching his limbs in that elegant way
Is something he can't do, not even today"

Now, quietly listening to all of this craziness
About the lion king's supposed laziness
Was the wisest old owl perched high in the tree

"Why didn't you animals come and ask me?
I've heard and listened to all that you've said
About who should be allowed the crown on his head

You said you want someone who is strong, brave and bold
With a beautiful coat that looks like spun gold

And you want an animal who's always the winner
When he's out late at night stalking his dinner
This king that you choose must never lose!
But that's not all. Of course, there's more
The animal king needs a loud, scary roar

He must walk brave and tall, filled with pride
With a long and elegant stretched-out stride

Now does that sound like a
king I've described?"

"Yes!" shouted the animals
their eyes fixed on the owl

Then suddenly they jumped
When they heard a loud growl

"This king you've described sounds just like me,"
purred the lion from behind the tree

"I know you all think in the day I'm lazy
But you would be too, if you were the king
Spending the nights hunting and prowling
Plotting and planning on who's the best dinner
This one, not that one - he looks much thinner

And when I'm tired and just want to rest
I still stand tall and push out my chest
My hair is golden, my roar is the loudest
And in this land, I'm the strongest and proudest!"

They stared at him. They heard his voice
The job he had was not his choice

Elephant, giraffe and baboon's little child
curtsied and bowed and then bent to the ground

The animals were silent, not one made a sound
They all stood there frozen, then looked up from the ground

Suddenly they sang out in a unified voice:

"We have our king. We've made our choice!

Lion stays king! Let's honour him
From the hilltops his praises we'll shout out and sing

Here's to the lion, our chosen king!"

First published by Jacana Media (Pty) Ltd in 2012

10 Orange Street
Sunnyside
Auckland Park 2092
South Africa
(+27 11) 628-3200
www.jacana.co.za

In collaboration with 2sq Design (Pty) Ltd
© Text: Tina Scotford, 2012
© Illustrations: Frans Groenewald, 2012

ISBN 978-1-4314-0693-7

Editor: Dominique Herman
Designer: Jeannie Coetzee
Set in DK Crayon Crumble 22 pt
Job no. 001811
Printed by Tien Wah Press (Pte) Ltd

See a complete list of Jacana titles at www.jacana.co.za